This book belongs to:

_ _ _ _ _ _ _ _ _ _ _

To Callum and Lily xx – M.R.

For my super studio mates, silly sausages all! – T.F.

··· INGREDIENTS ···

Ⓐ

This paperback edition first published in Great Britain in 2019 by Andersen Press Ltd.

First published in Great Britain in 2018 by Andersen Press Ltd., 20 Vauxhall Bridge Road, London SW1V 2SA.

Printed and bound in China.

1 3 5 7 9 10 8 6 4 2

British Library Cataloguing in Publication Data available.

ISBN 978 1 78344 751 0

ZING
Best Sea Salt

Ten fat sausages, sizzling in a pan.
One went POP and the other went...

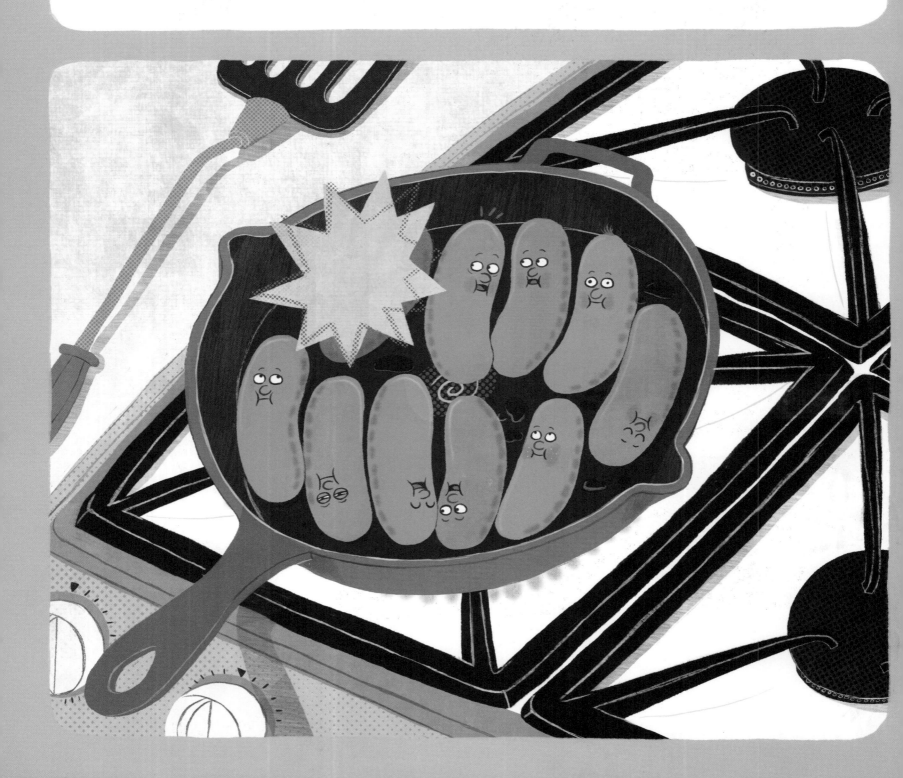

Hang on a minute!
I do not like this.
The fridge went hummm,
but the pan goes hissss.
Well, I won't go BANG
and I won't go POP.

And Sausage Number Two went hop, hop, hop.

Over the counter and glug, glug, glug!

He was doing quite well till they pulled out the plug.

He spluttered and reached for the chain.
But Sausage Number Two
WHOOSHED straight down the drain.

Eight fat sausages, sizzling in a pan.
One went POP and the other went...

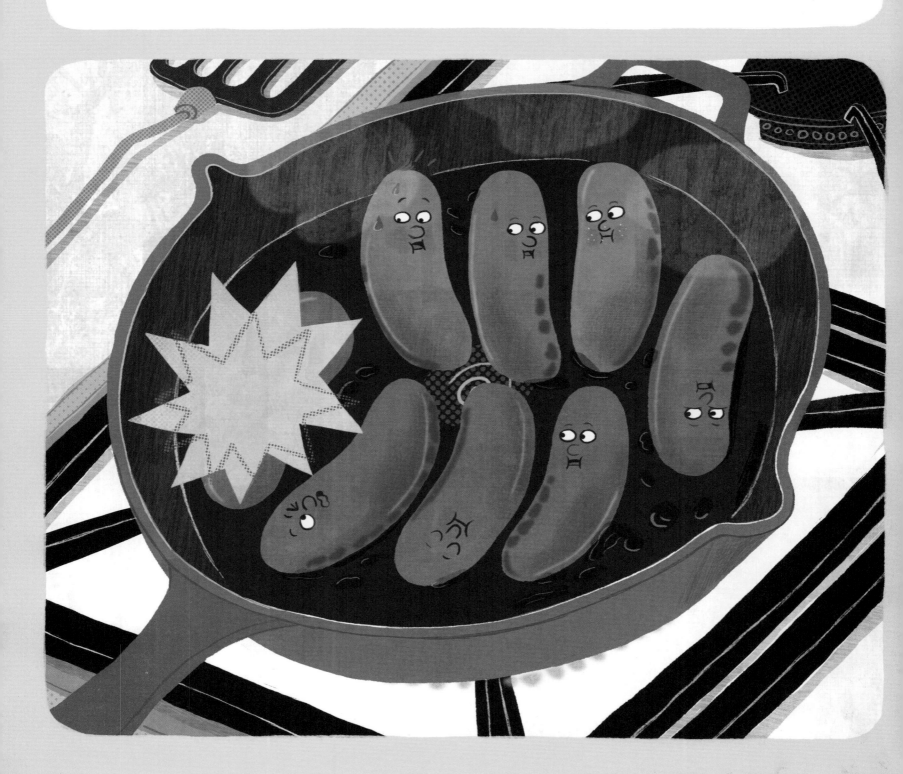

HANG on a minute! I've had quite enough of sitting around in this hot, oily stuff. Well, I won't go BANG and I won't go POP.

And Sausage Number Four went hop, hop, hop.

Over the counter
and into a bowl.
"This is more comfortable."

"Yes, on the whole
I am far better off.
But this switch is a mystery..."

Six fat sausages, sizzling in a pan.
One went POP and the other went...

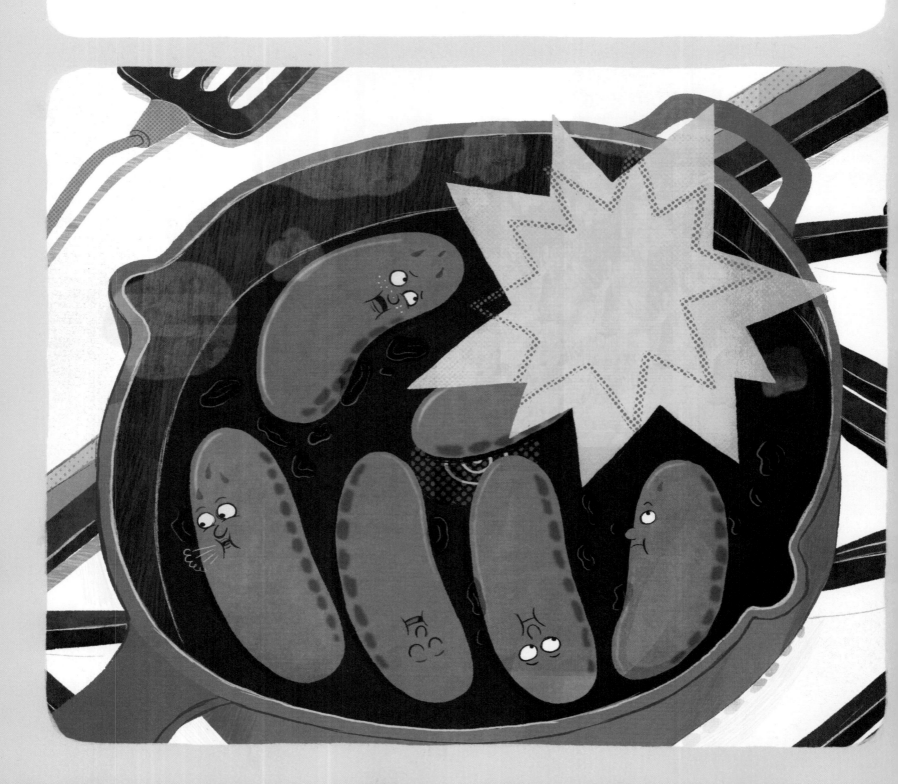

HANG on a minute, I want to break free! I don't want to end up as somebody's tea. Well, I won't go BANG and I won't go POP.

And Sausage Number Six went hop, hop, hop.

Straight up the cookbooks and onto the fridge.

Over the wide open Freezer Top Ridge.

"The whole world awaits,
I'm a freewheeling man.
GIDDY UP!"
Sausage Six was
flung by the fan.

Four fat sausages, sizzling in a pan.
One went POP and the other went...

HANG on a minute, that was my best friend. She didn't deserve such a terrible end. Well, I won't go bang and I won't go pop.

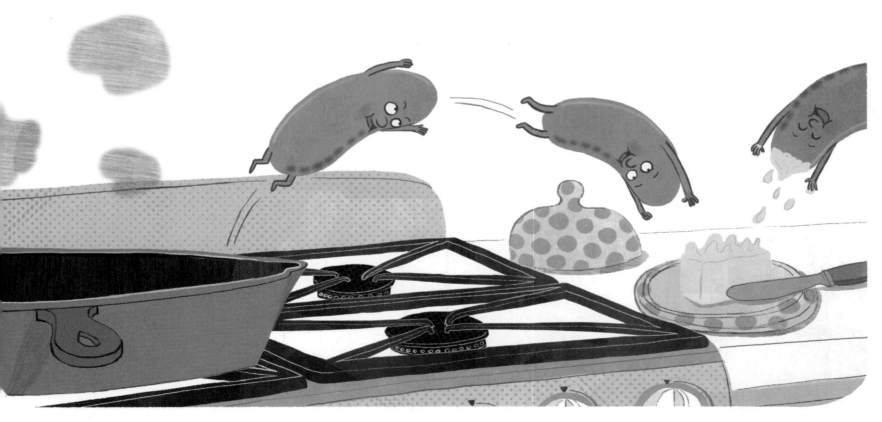

And Sausage Number Eight went hop, hop, hop.

Down from the counter and over the floor.

Past the cat's bed.
"If I just reach the door..."

Two fat sausages, sizzling in a pan.
"Try not to POP. We'll escape – I've a plan."

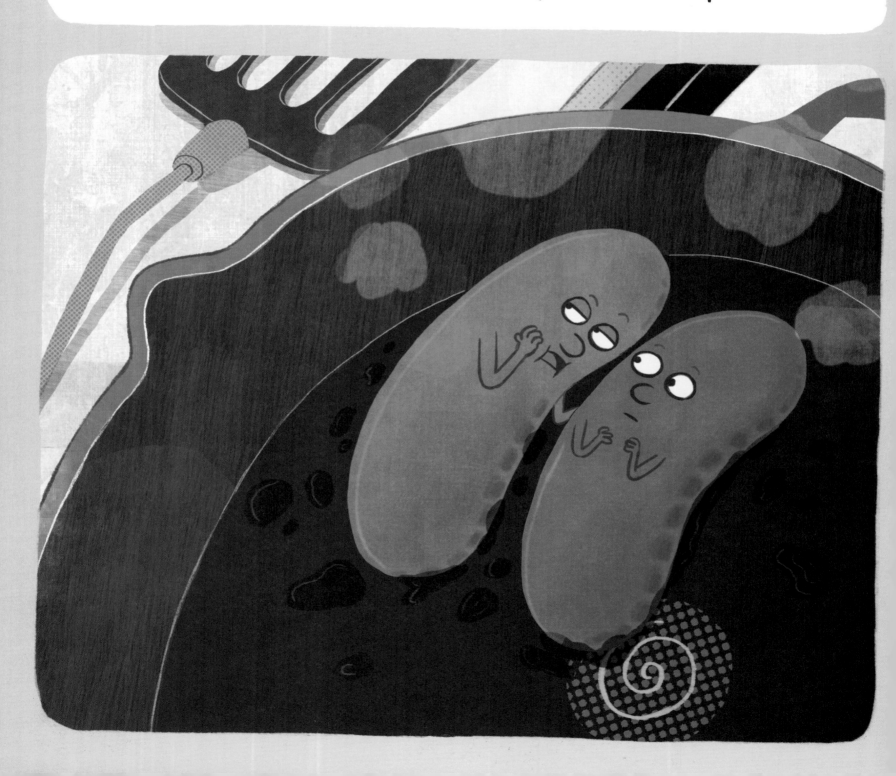

BANG!

yelled the sausage,
and

POP!

said his brother.

The hob was switched off.
They embraced one another.
Now, as sausages go,
that last plan was quite clever.
Might this pair survive?

Over the counter they went at a run.
"Let's hide in this squishy thing. Whee! This is fun!"
They hulaed in onion rings, danced in red sauce.
Two silly sausages...